A Titanic Friendship

★ Also by ★
Debbie Dadey

MERMAID TALES

Mermaid Tales

★ Debbie Dadey ★

Illustrated by
Tatevik Avakyan

BOOK 22

A Titanic Friendship

ALADDIN
NEW YORK   LONDON   TORONTO   SYDNEY   NEW DELHI

ALADDIN

An imprint of Simon & Schuster Children's Publishing Division

1230 Avenue of the Americas, New York, New York 10020

First Aladdin paperback edition June 2022

Text copyright © 2022 by Debbie Dadey

Illustrations copyright © 2022 by Tatevik Avakyan

Also available in an Aladdin hardcover edition.

All rights reserved, including the right of reproduction in whole or in part in any form.

ALADDIN and related logo are registered trademarks of Simon & Schuster, Inc.

For information about special discounts for bulk purchases, please contact Simon & Schuster Special Sales at 1-866-506-1949 or business@simonandschuster.com.

The Simon & Schuster Speakers Bureau can bring authors to your live event.

For more information or to book an event contact the Simon & Schuster Speakers Bureau at 1-866-248-3049 or visit our website at www.simonspeakers.com.

Cover designed by Alicia Mikles

Interior designed by Michael Rosamilia

The text of this book was set in BelucianNG.

Manufactured in the United States of America 0522 OFF

2 4 6 8 10 9 7 5 3 1

Library of Congress Cataloging-in-Publication Data

Names: Dadey, Debbie, author. | Avakyan, Tatevik, 1983- illustrator. | Dadey, Debbie. Mermaid tales ; 22.

Title: A Titanic friendship / Debbie Dadey ; illustrated by Tatevik Avakyan.

Description: First Aladdin paperback edition. | New York : Aladdin, 2022. | Series: Mermaid tales ; 22 | Audience: Ages 6 to 9. | Summary: Echo's third grade class visit the Titanic and figure out a way of including their new classmate, Anita, who is confined to a wheeled chair.

Identifiers: LCCN 2021046641 (print) | LCCN 2021046642 (ebook) | ISBN 9781534457355 (paperback) | ISBN 9781534457362 (hardcover) | ISBN 9781534457379 (ebook)

Subjects: LCSH: Titanic (Steamship)—Juvenile fiction. | Mermaids—Juvenile fiction. | People with disabilities—Juvenile fiction. | Friendship—Juvenile fiction. | School field trips—Juvenile fiction. | CYAC: Titanic (Steamship)—Fiction. | Mermaids—Fiction. | People with disabilities—Fiction. | Friendship—Fiction. | School field trips—Fiction. | LCGFT: Novels.

Classification: LCC PZ7.D128 Ti 2022 (print) | LCC PZ7.D128 (ebook) | DDC [Fic]—dc23

LC record available at https://lccn.loc.gov/2021046641

LC ebook record available at https://lccn.loc.gov/2021046642

For Alex

Contents

Ship Eating

WHAT IS A BACTERIUM that eats ships?" Mrs. Karp asked.

Rocky Ridge shook his head. "Little bitty bacteria can't do that. Their stomachs would explode!"

Echo Reef had to agree with Rocky.

★ 1 ★

Her third-grade class had just started studying them, but she was sure her teacher had said something about bacteria being really, really small. Since they'd started their lessons, Echo scrubbed carefully every night. She didn't want to think about icky bacteria or their cousins, archaea, on her pretty pink tail.

Echo's merfriend Kiki Coral raised her hand slowly. "Doesn't it depend on whether the ship is wood or steel?"

"Why would that matter?" Pearl Swamp asked.

Mrs. Karp grinned. "Actually, it makes a big difference. Some bacteria like to eat wood, and some eat steel. In fact, over the next week we will be studying different types of bacteria and creating paintings of large clusters of them in art class."

Painting sounded a lot better than doing a big report. Echo would have to learn about the different types. How many could there be?

"The bacteria *H. titanicae* is named after the steel ship it has been eating for about a hundred years," Mrs. Karp told them. "Does anyone recognize that name?"

Echo's hand shot in the air. "Are you telling me that something is eating the most famous ship ever? The *Titanic*?" Echo loved everything about humans, and that particular ship was legendary.

"It's true." Mrs. Karp nodded. "In fact, in twenty years it may be completely gone."

"No wavy way!" Echo said in disbelief.

"Let's get rid of that tica-tockie bacteria!" Rocky urged.

"It's called *H. titanicae*," Kiki said. "The H is for 'Halomonas.'"

"Isn't there a way to stop the bacteria?" Echo's good merfriend Shelly Siren asked.

Mrs. Karp shrugged. "I'm not sure we should. It's the way of nature."

Echo couldn't believe it. She'd read about the fabulous human ship that had been like a floating palace. People had thought it couldn't be sunk, but sadly it had—on its first voyage! How could the whole thing be disappearing?

"But luckily we'll get to see it before it's gone," Mrs. Karp announced. "We will go on an ocean trip to visit it next week."

Several kids gasped, but Echo couldn't help squealing. Were they really going to visit the *Titanic*? It was a dream come true!

2

New Merkid

ECHO WAS STILL THINKING about the *Titanic* later after Tail Flippers practice. "Did you hear the exciting news?" Pearl said as she floated over to Echo. They were in the middle of MerPark's biggest kelp field.

"Yes!" Echo said. "I'm so excited about the ocean trip!"

Pearl frowned and twisted her long pearl necklace. "Who cares about visiting a rusty old ship? I'm talking about the new merstudent!"

"We're getting a new merkid in our class? How do you know?"

Wanda Slug swam up beside Pearl. "I overheard Mrs. Karp talking with Headmaster Hermit when we went to the cafeteria. Isn't it shelltacular?"

"Fins crossed for a cute merboy!" Pearl giggled.

"Maybe he'll want to join the Tail Flippers team," Wanda agreed. "We need a new top person." Wanda had just recently been added to the team herself.

"I'm usually the top person on the pyramids," Echo said. But Pearl and Wanda had already splashed away to chat with other Tail Flippers about the new merstudent.

Echo overheard lots of comments like "I heard he's from the Northern Oceans!" and "I hope she'll sit by me."

Pearl said, "Maybe the new merkid will be able to do the Scale Dropper really well!"

Echo had heard quite enough. The Scale Dropper was her favorite flip! It sounded like her whole team was ready to replace her. How she wished her merfriends Kiki and Shelly were on the team.

Echo grabbed her book bag and headed home, but at the last minute she made a slight detour toward the Trident City Library, swerving around the Trident Academy manta ray bus outside. She wanted to do extra research on the *Titanic*. She sailed past the marble pillars that lined the entrance to the oldest library in the mer-world. Echo barely glanced at the pink marble walls and the sparkling diamond pictures on the ceiling. She knew just where to go inside the big space, although usually one or two of her buddies were with her. She'd looked at the ship books many times. Human things were fin-tastic, and ships were the biggest human things ever!

Echo swished to a stop in front of several empty shelves. Every single *Titanic* book was gone!

3

Mean Merstudent

AMERGIRL ABOUT ECHO'S age sat at a table covered with books. They were all about the *Titanic*! The stranger turned a kelp page in the biggest one.

Echo frowned. It wasn't right to take all the books on one subject. "Excuse me, do you mind if I borrow a couple of these?" She'd already read her school's single volume three times over.

The mergirl pushed back her brown braid with her bright orange fingernails. "Are you going on the *Titanic* ocean trip?"

Echo grinned. "Yes, I've always wanted to go. I just want two books. You can have the rest."

The mergirl raised an eyebrow before shaking her head. "No."

Echo couldn't believe it. How rude! She wanted to shout at the mergirl, but instead she swirled around. Echo flipped her tail just enough to make a wave, hoping it caused the meanie to lose her place.

She was still mad about it the next morning when she was swimming to school with Shelly. "She had every book about the *Titanic* and wouldn't share!"

"Is she an older merstudent?" Shelly asked.

They didn't see the bigger students at Trident Academy often, but Echo surely would have recognized the mergirl. "No," Echo said as they swam into their school's main entrance hall. She stopped so suddenly Shelly smashed into her.

"Ouch, why'd you stop?"

"That's her! It's the mean mergirl I told you about." Echo pointed to a large group of merkids surrounding the brown-haired mergirl. She even had a stack of books on her orange lap. Echo was pretty sure they were the *Titanic* books from the library, and it made her mad all over again.

"What is she sitting on?" Shelly asked.

Echo took her eyes away from the books and tried to figure out the strange chair. What kind of seat had big yellow wheels and fins? "It must be a human invention," Echo said.

Echo forgot all about the mean mergirl when the conch sounded for classes to begin and everyone scurried to their rooms. She was pulling her homework out of her bag when in rolled the new merstudent.

Echo slapped her homework on her desk

as Mrs. Karp said, "Class, please welcome our newest member. Anita Bloom joins us from the Southern Oceans. Shelly and Kiki, please scoot your desks over to make room."

Automatically everyone rose and said, "Hello, Anita." Echo mumbled it.

Anita's face turned a bright red. Without a word she rolled her chair past Echo. "I hope you are enjoying those books," Echo snapped.

Anita jerked her head up before sneering, "Actually, they're great."

Echo reached to pass her homework to the front of the room. But it was missing! That's when she saw her carefully done math paper on the floor. It was covered with dirty tire marks! Anita had ruined her homework on purpose!

Titanic Dream

NAME A BACTERIUM THAT can cause your skin to itch," Mrs. Karp asked her class later that morning.

Anita's hand shot up in the water. "*Oscillatoria willei.*"

Rocky frowned. "O-lotty-whaty?"

Mrs. Karp nodded at Anita. "Very good. Can anyone tell me the nickname for *Oscillatoria willei*?"

Anita bit her lip like she wanted to answer, but Kiki raised her hand. "Wasn't it once known as blue-green algae?"

"Exactly," Mrs. Karp said. Anita gave Kiki a tails-up signal. What was that about? Surely the mean mergirl hadn't made a pal of Kiki already. They'd barely met!

Echo couldn't believe her bad luck when Anita parked her chair at the polished granite lunch table she always shared with Shelly and Kiki. It was their special time together. "What's going on?" Echo asked.

Kiki grinned from her spot beside Anita.

"My new roommate is joining us for lunch. Isn't that great?"

"Roommate?" Echo said, with a sinking feeling in her stomach. Did everyone like Anita better? After all, the Tail Flippers had been quick to want to replace her. Were her best merbuddies next?

"I have that big room, and since Wanda isn't my roommate anymore, I had plenty of space," Kiki said.

"It's an awesome room," Anita said. "I love the waterfall and your killer-whale bed."

Shelly floated over to the table with two trays full of crab casserole and barnacle buns. She placed one in front of Anita. "Thanks," Anita said.

Shelly grinned. "I can get it every day for you if you'd like." Echo couldn't believe it. Not only was the girl mean, she'd stolen Kiki for a merfriend and was having Shelly get lunch for her!

Anita shook her head. "No, I will be more used to things tomorrow. But it was nice of you to get it for me today."

"Nice!" Echo shrieked and pointed at Anita. "You were not nice when you took all the *Titanic* books at the public library and wouldn't even let me look at one." Shelly and Echo gasped at Echo's loud shout.

"What is all the screaming about?" Pearl frowned as she floated near their table.

Anita's cheeks turned red. "It's my fault.

I wasn't very kind yesterday. I was jealous of Echo."

Echo put her hands on her pink hips. "Why would you be jealous of me?" After all, everyone seemed to like Anita better than her.

Anita shrugged. "You get to go on the ocean trip, and I can't."

"Why not?" Shelly asked.

"My wheeled chair is a great human invention, and I'm lucky it was found. But even though it can float, I still can't go around tight corners and in the tiny hallways of a crumbling ship," Anita explained.

Echo wiggled her perfectly working fins. She had hurt her tail once and remembered how it had been really hard to get around. Echo had been jealous of Anita before she'd even met her and couldn't help feeling bad about it.

"That's not fair," Kiki said. "I'm surprised Mrs. Karp would plan an ocean trip that you can't go on."

Anita shook her head. "It's not her fault. This trip was scheduled before I came."

"If you can't go," Shelly told her, "then none of us should go."

"Fine with me," Pearl said. "I don't want to go on a broken old ship anyway. They give me the creeps."

Echo couldn't believe it! Her dream of visiting the *Titanic* was disappearing. She had to do something fast!

Boycott

WHAT'S A BOYCOTT?" ROCKY asked when they were back in the classroom.

"It's where we refuse to do or buy something because we don't believe in it," Kiki explained.

Echo groaned. She usually liked how

smart Kiki was, but not today.

"Why would we boycott the *Titanic* trip?" Adam asked. "I want to go. An ocean trip is much better than math practice!"

Shelly scrunched her nose at Adam. "We shouldn't go on the trip because it's not fair. If one of us can't go, then none of us should."

Rocky frowned at Anita. "This is all her fault!"

Anita gasped. "I never said you shouldn't go."

"It's nobody's fault," Kiki snapped. "When Mrs. Karp gets back into the classroom, we are going to tell her we don't want this ocean trip."

More groans sounded from around the

classroom, but Pearl shrugged. "It's just a stinky old ship."

Echo plopped her head onto her desk. The crab casserole swirled in her stomach, and she felt sick. When Mrs. Karp swished into the room, Echo rushed up to her. "I need to visit the nurse's office."

Rocky teased, "Don't throw up on me!"

Mrs. Karp took one look at her and nodded. Echo dashed down the hall before Kiki could tell their teacher about the boycott. Nurse Dilly Dally DoDo gave Echo some Cornish kelp crackers to settle her tummy and made her lie down.

In a few minutes her stomach felt better, but her brain was still upset. Echo really, really wanted to see the *Titanic*. She'd even dreamed of seeing the famous ship with the grand staircase and fancy wood paneling. What a shame that it had hit an iceberg and sunk so quickly. It wasn't fair that Anita couldn't go. It wasn't fair that Rocky was blaming Anita either. It was just a terrible mess!

"How about a joke to make you feel better?" Nurse DoDo asked, touching Echo's forehead with the tip of her bright-orange tail. "What did the shark say after eating the clown fish?"

Nurse DoDo loved to tell jokes to cheer up her patients, but Echo wasn't in the mood. She shrugged. "I don't know."

"This tastes a little funny." Nurse DoDo laughed at her own joke, and before Echo could stop her, she asked another. "How did the hammerhead do on his spelling test?"

Echo groaned. Spelling was her absolute worst subject.

Nurse DoDo laughed again. "He nailed it!"

"Nurse DoDo." Echo smiled at the tall, thin mermaid. "Remember when I hurt my tail and used crutches?"

Nurse DoDo nodded. "What I remember most is the miracle cream Pearl gave you that turned out to be a disaster cream."

"That was awful," Echo agreed. "But the crutches I used helped me until my tail healed. What do merpeople do if their tails won't work at all?"

"Ah, you are thinking of the new mer-student," Nurse DoDo said.

"Because of her my class is boycotting the *Titanic* ocean trip," Echo blurted. "It's not right that Anita can't go. But it won't

be fair if we can't either. Surely merfolk have figured out a way to help mermaids who can't swim."

Nurse DoDo scratched the purple stripe that ran down the middle of her bushy orange hair. "There have been some advancements using pufferfish floats. The results haven't been too encouraging though, especially if there are larger fish in the area. And apparently the pufferfish don't take direction very well."

Echo sighed. It wouldn't do for the pufferfish to be eaten by a tiger shark in the middle of their ocean trip or to swim away with Anita.

"I will send letters to my medical groups

asking for suggestions," Nurse DoDo told her.

"Thanks." Echo said. Even if the letters were sent by Manta Ray Express, answers might not come in time to save their *Titanic* trip. Echo would just have to find her own solution. If humans could come up with a wheeled chair, she could figure out something even better. She had to!

6

Solutions

"COME WITH ME," PEARL snapped as the last conch bell sounded to end the day.

Echo shook her head. "I'm going home." She had to figure out how to save the *Titanic* trip.

Pearl grabbed her arm and tugged her

toward the mergirls' dorm rooms. "If I have to go to this, then so do you."

"What are you talking about?" Echo asked.

"Wanda and some of the others are determined to figure out a way for Anita to go on the trip," Pearl said. "They are canceling the boycott."

Echo smiled. If everyone worked together,

surely they could come up with a solution. Echo's stomach suddenly felt much better.

"What's the big deal about an old boat?" Pearl complained. "I wish we could go on an ocean trip to a fashion show or at least an opera."

Things weren't going well in Anita and Kiki's dorm room. Shelly was shaking her head at Wanda. Kiki frowned at Wanda before saying, "That won't work!" Morgan was hoisting Anita up by a long scarf.

"What are you doing?" Echo asked Morgan.

"M-my aunt used a sling like this to carry around her b-baby," Morgan explained.

Pearl nodded. "My mom does the same thing with my new brother, Ray."

Anita glared at Morgan. "Thanks, but I am not a baby."

"Who cares?" Pearl said. "As long as it works." But it didn't.

"Oops!" Morgan cried out as Anita flipped out of the slinglike scarf and landed on her head.

"Ouch!" Anita squealed.

"Oh no!" Echo helped Anita back into her chair. "Are you all right?"

Anita rubbed her head. "Yes, but let's forget that idea."

"We need something safe," Kiki told the other mergirls. They tossed ideas back and forth, but Echo was distracted by the new additions to the dorm room. Normally Kiki's rather creepy killer-whale skeleton bed sat in the middle of the room, but it had been pushed to the side to make way for another strange bed.

"Is this yours?" Echo asked Anita.

Anita grinned. "I really like the *Titanic*."

Echo laughed. "I guess so." Anita's bed was a miniature ship with RMS *Titanic* written on the side. A life preserver and a captain's wheel were on either side of a fake porthole at the bow. The wall beside her bed was filled with kelp posters, one of them showing where all the rooms were on the *Titanic*. There was even a mosaic of the grand staircase!

No wonder Anita had been jealous that Echo would see the ship. If anyone in their class should visit the *Titanic*, it should definitely be the new mergirl. But looking at her merfriends arguing about solutions, Echo knew it wouldn't be easy!

Echo sighed as she floated through MerPark on her way home an hour later, carrying some of Anita's *Titanic* books. Echo's stomach felt better, but her head hurt. Lots of ways to help Anita go on the trip had been discussed—everything from a shell pulled by a dwarf sperm whale to a strange green-turtle backpack. None of the ideas sounded very hopeful.

"Watch out!" Rocky shouted as he rushed past on his orange sea horse, Zollie.

Suddenly Echo choked on seawater. "Rocky, wait!"

She had a great idea! But what if Anita hated it?

Rustycycle

WHY ARE YOU CRYING?"
Echo asked Anita.

Anita wiped a tear off her cheek. "I'm just so happy."

Echo grinned. She couldn't believe everything had worked out. It certainly hadn't been easy. First, she'd talked Rocky into letting Anita use one of his sea horses. Then it was tricky convincing Mrs. Karp to allow Anita to ride a sea horse on their ocean trip. Then Echo'd given Anita riding lessons, with Shelly lending a tail. Kiki had assisted with writing and sending a permission note to Anita's parents via the Manta Ray Super Express.

Even Mr. Fangtooth, the school custodian, had helped by making a special saddle. Echo was already planning a way for Anita to use a sea horse and saddle to be part of the Tail Flippers.

It had taken a lot of afternoons working together to get everything done on time. Echo'd learned a lot about the new merstudent. Surprisingly, Anita had a human collection just as big as hers. How could Echo have ever thought Anita was mean? Even though they'd become merfriends, all the work had been exhausting!

But it was worth it because they were now floating in the chilly waters in front of the huge sunken ship, the RMS *Titanic*. Actually, most of the class was floating while Anita was riding Pinky. She was the small mate of Zollie, Rocky's favorite sea horse.

"Why does she get to ride and I have to swim?" Rocky complained. "My tail's worn out!"

Shelly shook her finger at him. "Rocky, you know Anita can't swim. Stop being so crabby."

Rocky shrugged. "Sorry, Anita, I'm just tired." Most of the trip had been on a large manta ray, but it had been an extremely long and cold swim from the nearest Manta Ray Express Station. Mrs. Karp had warned them it would be chilly, and luckily everyone had bundled up. Echo was sure her nose was turning red from the frigid water.

Mrs. Karp clapped her hands and ignored her class's grumbles. "Now, students. This is a sunken ship."

Rocky rolled his eyes. Echo had to admit, it was a silly thing for their teacher to say. After all, the amazing wreck towered over them. Even in the dark waters, a large rail was visible on the top deck. This was the biggest human vessel Echo had ever seen, even though the ocean floor around Trident City was littered with many of them, of all sizes.

"We must respect it," Mrs. Karp continued. "Do not touch anything. We are here to observe the bacteria, as well as any other ocean creatures you may find."

Pearl sniffed. "Bacteria are so disgusting."

"Most bacteria are good," Kiki told Pearl. "You have about a hundred trillion good bacteria in your body."

Pearl and Wanda squealed. "That's not true!" Wanda shouted.

Mrs. Karp chuckled. "Actually, it is, but we'll study that later. Right now, let's concentrate on what we view on this ship."

Shelly raised her hand. "I thought bacteria were too little to see."

Mrs. Karp smiled. "You are right. But there are large clusters that will be visible, including the rusticles."

"What's a rustycycle?" Adam spouted.

Mrs. Karp pointed to the icicle-like strands of rust that covered most of the ship. "The rusticles are made up of twenty-seven different kinds of bacteria, including *H. titanicae*. Just remember not to touch them, because they are very delicate."

"Everyone must stay with their buddies," she continued. "Now listen carefully. If you see a bright light, you must evacuate immediately. We will meet behind the stern of the ship over there." Mrs. Karp pointed to the broken rear half of the huge vessel.

"That's what's left of the poop deck." Rocky snickered.

Mrs. Karp frowned. "We will have no joking around. This is a place for quiet and reflection. After all, in nearly every sunken ship, lives were lost."

Echo felt a shiver go down her back, and it had nothing to do with the cold water around them. She swam closer to her assigned buddy, Anita.

"W-what kind of light are you talking about?" Morgan asked.

"Human light. They can't see in the dark as well as merfolk, and they have been known to visit this ship," Mrs. Karp explained. "It's highly unlikely. Still, any bright light means we must get away quickly. I will be on the alert while you study the bacteria."

Pearl groaned. "I can't believe I have to go into a creepy old ship."

"Cheer up," Anita said. "Maybe you'll find the missing necklace."

Pearl swirled around to look at Anita. "What are you talking about?"

Echo winked at Anita. "There's a legend about a fabulous necklace being left behind on the *Titanic*. It's supposed to be the most beautiful piece of jewelry ever made."

Pearl grinned and touched her pearl necklace. "Well, what are we waiting for? Let's get on that ship!"

A Reason to Shout

ECHO FINISHED SKETCHING A particularly large collection of rusticles hanging on the top deck. It was like a fancy sculpture or a beautiful waterfall. How could it be made of bacteria? Ick! "Let's go. Mrs. Karp is taking everyone inside," she suggested to Anita.

Anita nodded before whispering, "Do you think we should tell Pearl there's probably no truth to the legend about a missing necklace?"

Echo glanced at Pearl as their class disappeared into a dark hallway. "I doubt she'd even believe us. She'd most likely think we were looking for it ourselves."

Anita shrugged. "Come on. I can't wait to get inside." It was a good thing Pinky was a small sea horse, because part of the hallway was filled with piles of sand and rusticles hanging along the walls. Doors hung open or were missing, allowing them to glimpse inside rooms. One had a strange white bowl, large enough for a merperson to fit inside. Another had a bright shiny thing Mrs. Karp called a clock.

"W-why are there so many holes on the side of the ship?" Morgan asked. "Is that why it sank?"

"Those were windows. The first-class passengers could see the water from them," Anita said.

"It's a ship," Rocky told them. "Everyone could see the ocean."

"Not according to some reports," Anita said. "Some passengers were at the bottom of the ship and never saw the water."

"How awful," Echo said. Why would humans do that? Were they afraid of the ocean?

"Yikes!" Pearl shrieked and grabbed

Shelly's arm. "Did you see that shark? It went right past that window!"

Echo gulped. "What kind was it?"

"What difference does it make?" Pearl squealed.

"The difference between being a snack and being ignored," Kiki told her.

Mrs. Karp clapped her hands. "How wonderful! That was a Greenland shark. They are rarely spotted."

"I wish I had seen it," Rocky said, leaning out the window.

"What if it's hungry?" Wanda hid behind Shelly and Pearl.

"Don't worry," Kiki told the class. "A Greenland shark hasn't attacked a merperson in over a hundred years."

"All right, class, let's finish moving through the officers' quarters to where a smokestack used to be. There should be plenty of rusticles to see there," Mrs. Karp said. "After that we'll go to the radio room and the grand staircase."

"What's a radio?" Shelly asked.

"Mrs. Karp!" Rocky yelled, interrupting Shelly.

"Rocky," Mrs. Karp said, "there's no need to shout. We're all right here."

Rocky pointed out the window. "Actually, there's a big reason to scream. And it's coming our way!"

"What is it?" Pearl shuddered.

"Is it another one of those creepy Greenland sharks?"

"No," Rocky said, his eyes wide. "It's something worse. Much worse!"

Before Rocky could explain, a bright light blasted onto one side of the *Titanic*. "What is that?" Echo gasped.

Anita clutched Pinky's reins tightly. "Humans!"

Hiding

WE'RE TRAPPED!" WANDA shrieked.

Mrs. Karp quickly shouted orders. "Put your back against the hall wall on this side. Do not get near the doors." The merkids scrunched together on the wall in between two doorways, making sure their tails weren't visible. The bright light flashed through the window, past the open door, and onto the far wall. As long as they stayed put, the humans couldn't see them.

Morgan began crying, along with several other merkids. "They're going to catch us, and I'll never see my home again."

Echo gulped. She'd always wanted to see a human, but she didn't want to be caught! If the humans came inside the ship, they were sunk! They needed a room big enough to hide in, away from prying human eyes. There was no way they could make it to the stern wreckage now without being seen.

Shelly and Mrs. Karp peeked into rooms

on the opposite side of the ship from the light. "They all have windows!" Shelly said.

Echo grabbed Anita's arm. "Anita, you had a diagram of the *Titanic* hanging on your dorm room wall. Is there a place where we can hide?"

Anita bit her lip before suddenly flashing a big smile. "Yes!" As soon as the bright light moved to a different section of the ship, Anita led the entire class to a lower level and then another. Echo lost count of how deep they were going.

"Do you know where you're going?" Pearl asked. "At least on the first

floor, we could have escaped easier."

Anita paused in front of a curtain of rusticles. "This is it."

"Where are we?" Mrs. Karp asked.

"This is called the potato room. It should be large enough for all of us," Anita said.

"Do humans eat potato fish?" Adam asked, but no one answered.

"There's no door," Rocky snapped. "How can we hide?"

"If there was a door, it would probably be torn off or rusted shut," Kiki told him.

"This is what I was hoping for," Anita said. "If we can get inside without touching the rusticles, we should be quite hidden."

It wasn't easy, but they managed to glide past the fragile bacteria without breaking any of the long strands. They huddled inside the small windowless room. The rusticles hid them completely. It was the darkest place Echo had ever been in. She held her hand up in front of her face but couldn't see her fingers move. Several merkids whimpered. "Now what do we do?" Kiki whispered.

"We wait in silence," Mrs. Karp commanded.

Immediately the crying stopped. Echo was surprised no one could hear her heart thumping when a light flashed outside the room. It wasn't as bright as before, so it wasn't too close. Still, Echo could feel Anita and Pinky tense beside her. Was everyone holding their breath? Echo sure was. After a few minutes, the light moved on and then disappeared altogether.

They waited and waited. Then they waited even longer. Echo's tail was so cramped she could hardly feel her fins. "Can we leave now?" Pearl finally whispered.

"Let me check. Everyone stay put." Mrs. Karp slipped outside the room.

Echo crossed her tail fins for luck. What if something happened to Mrs. Karp?

In the Dark

MRS. KARP DIDN'T COME back.

"W-what are we going to do?" Morgan sobbed. Even in the dark, Echo could tell who was speaking.

"We'll never find our way back to the Manta Ray Express Station without

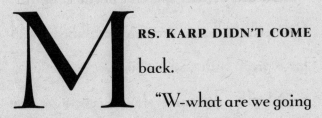

Mrs. Karp," Wanda said with a shaky voice.

"Maybe she got eaten by that Greenland shark," Adam muttered.

"Or humans," Rocky said.

"Humans don't eat merpeople," Kiki snapped.

"How do you know?" Adam teased. "Have you ever met one?" Several merkids wailed like it was the end of the ocean. If Echo could have seen Adam, she would have given him a mean look.

"Maybe someone should go look for Mrs. Karp," Rocky suggested.

"I'll do it," Pearl said. "I'm not going to wait around here until the bacteria start eating us."

Now Echo felt like crying, even though she was pretty sure the ship's bacteria weren't going to gobble up her tail. "No," she said. "We should wait a little longer."

Shelly agreed. "Mrs. Karp told us to stay put."

"I'll give her a few more merminutes," Pearl told them. "And then I'm going out there."

"I'm freezing," Wanda complained. "My fins are turning into an ice sculpture."

"It's so crowded in here, I can barely breathe," someone complained.

"This sea horse is taking up way too much room," Adam muttered.

"Let's think of something else," Echo

suggested. "What's your favorite part of the *Titanic* so far?"

"I liked the big chains," Rocky said. "If I had one right now, I could tie up that shark."

"My favorite part will be getting out of here," Wanda said.

"Th-this is awful," Morgan whispered. "I-I'm going to have nightmares."

"This is a nightmare," Adam said firmly.

"I know a *Titanic* song," Anita said. "It's a new tune by the Rays." A couple of mer-girls squealed at the mention of the good-looking merboy band.

"How does it go?" Shelly asked.

"I think I can remember it," Anita said. "It's something like this . . .

"Humans built the ship Titanic, to sail the ocean blue.

"For they thought it was a ship that water would never go through.

"It was on its maiden trip, that an iceberg hit the ship.

"It was sad when the great ship went down."

"Quiet!" Pearl interrupted.

"That's rude," Shelly said. "I want to hear the rest."

"No, I heard a noise behind the curtain," Pearl told them.

It was true. Something was coming. Whatever it was, it was getting closer!

Scare

ECHO HELD HER BREATH. Whatever was out there had stopped. Was it a shark? A human?

"Class, it's safe. Come on out," Mrs. Karp announced.

Screams of relief filled the potato room.

"We're going to live!" shouted Rocky as everyone floated out into a small hallway.

Echo could barely move her tail. They had come so close to being discovered by humans. Stories of merfolk disappearing and never being seen again flowed through her head. She reached out and squeezed Pearl's hand. She gave Shelly and Kiki a hug.

Anita and Pinky floated away from everyone. Anita's face was pale. Was she all right? Before Echo could ask, Mrs. Karp announced, "In light of our recent scare, we will cut our trip short."

Some merkids clapped, but a few groaned. Mrs. Karp continued with a strict voice, "We will stay close together and swim past the grand staircase. Then we will head toward the Manta Ray station. Under no circumstances will anyone leave our group. Is that understood?"

Everyone nodded quickly before Mrs. Karp held up a hand. "Before we go, we need to thank the merperson who saved us. Without her quick thinking and knowledge, this could have ended differently. Thank you, Anita. We're so glad you joined our class and this trip."

Everyone swirled around to look at Anita and Pinky. Anita's face turned red while Pinky nodded her head like she was agreeing with Mrs. Karp. "Cheers for Anita!" Shelly called.

"Hip, hip, hooray!" Rocky yelled. Then

the entire merclass joined in with him, "Hip, hip, hooray!"

Shelly, Echo, and Kiki glided over to surround Anita and Pinky. "You saved us," Shelly said, giving Anita a pat on her tail.

"And to think you weren't even supposed to come," Kiki agreed. "It's lucky for us that Rocky let you ride Pinky." Pinky neighed at her name, and the mergirls laughed.

Anita looked at Echo and said, "It's lucky someone cared enough to find a way for me to come on the trip. Thanks to all of you."

"At first, I only did it so we could go," Echo admitted. "But now I realize merfriends don't leave merfriends behind, just like you didn't abandon us today to save yourself."

"I would never do that!" Anita gasped.

Echo gave her new buddy a hug. "I know, and that's why you're our merfriend."

Anita grinned. "Come on, let's go see that grand staircase!"

Class Reports
★ ✦ ★

BLUE-GREEN ALGAE

by Shelly Siren

If you feel something slimy in the water, get away from it!

It could be blue-green algae, and it can make you sick.

SEA SAWDUST

by Echo Reef

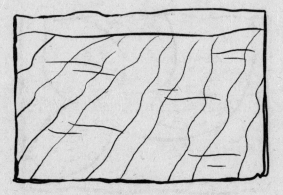

Sea sawdust has the fancy name *Trichodesmium*, but it can be seen in the water as brown stripes. It is usually a harmless bacterium, but there are lots of different brown algae. Some can be eaten, but some will make you very sick. Stay away, just in case!

VIBRIO VULNIFICUS

by Rocky Ridge

Mrs. Karp said I could draw a picture of what this bacterium does. It makes painful red swollen spots on your tail. Luckily, it is very rare that this bacterium hurts merpeople, but if it happens—get to a doctor fast! One book said that humans should never go in the ocean if they have a cut.

ALIIVIBRIO FISCHERI
by Kiki Coral

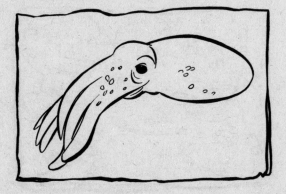

If you've ever seen a Hawaiian bobtail squid's blue-green glowing light, then you've seen this bacterium in action.

Without bacteria, the squid wouldn't glow!

MARINE SNOW
by Pearl Swamp

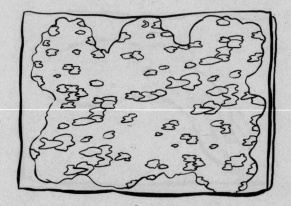

I thought this would be fun to learn about, but I was wrong. The snowlike flakes falling in the ocean are actually poop from phytoplankton and bacteria, along with little dead creatures! How disgusting!

H. TITANICAE
by Anita Bloom

My favorite bacterium is *H. titanicae*. It comes together to make amazing orange strands called rusticles to decorate old metal ships. Unfortunately, it also eats those ships!

The Mermaid Song
Mermaid Tales

REFRAIN:

Let the water roar

Deep down we're swimming along

Twirling, swirling, singing the mermaid song.

VERSE 1:

Shelly flips her tail

Racing, diving, chasing a whale

Twirling, swirling, singing the mermaid song.

VERSE 2:

Pearl likes to shine
Oh my Neptune, she looks so fine
Twirling, swirling, singing the mermaid song.

VERSE 3:

Shining Echo flips her tail
Backward, forward, without fail
Twirling, swirling, singing the mermaid song.

VERSE 4:

Amazing Kiki
Far from home and floating so free
Twirling, swirling, singing the mermaid song.

Author's Note

The RMS *Titanic* was believed to be unsinkable when it left England over a hundred years ago on its first voyage. Sadly, the *Titanic* hit an iceberg in such a way that it began sinking. Strangely enough, if it had hit the iceberg head-on, the ship would have taken longer to sink. The Rays song from Chapter Eleven is part of a folk song written by William and Versey Smith in 1915.

There actually was a potato room on the *Titanic*, filled with forty tons of potatoes. The ship was almost as long as three football fields and as tall as a seventeen-story building. In today's money, the most expensive ticket would cost $99,000!

Robert Ballard and his team found the wreckage of the great ship in 1985. They used underwater vehicles and a tiny submarine (like what shines the bright light in this story) to visit the wreck. The ship had broken into two parts. The stern (or back) had fallen apart, but the bow was still largely intact. Just recently, scientists have found that bacteria are slowly eating the ship. In less than twenty years, it is believed that the great *Titanic* will be only a rust spot on the bottom of the sea!

Anita's wheelchair idea is taken from one of the fun water types that are available today. Other amazing kinds are for using on the beach, skiing, skydiving, rock climbing, and hiking, and there are even wheelchairs for long scuba-diving trips. They are awesome!

Your friend,

Debbie Dadey

Glossary

BACTERIA: Bacteria are so small we can't see them, but they are everywhere. Most aren't dangerous, but a few can make us sick.

BARNACLE: Barnacles are related to crabs, lobsters, and shrimp. They stick to boats or even other sea creatures. They make one of the most powerful natural glues we know!

CONCH: Many sea snails go by this name, but "conch" usually refers to large snails that have a swirling shell.

CORNISH KELP: Many kinds of seaweed can be found off Cornish waters (in England) and are being used more and more in food.

CRAB: Crabs have no backbone and have a hard shell.

DWARF SPERM WHALE: This whale squirts out an inklike liquid to escape from enemies.

GREEN TURTLE: The large green turtle is also known as the black turtle or Pacific green turtle.

GREENLAND SHARK: This shark is one of the largest sharks and can live to be very old. Some reports say they live as long as four hundred years!

HAMMERHEAD SHARK: This shark's unusual hammer-shaped head is called a cephalofoil.

HAWAIIAN BOBTAIL SQUID: This squid lives near Hawaii and likes to bury itself in the sand. Bacteria help to camouflage it to look like the water around it at night.

JELLYFISH: Jellyfish squirt water from their mouths to move!

KILLER WHALE: Killer whales are the largest dolphins.

MANTA RAY: The giant manta ray is the largest ray and one of the largest fish in the ocean.

PEARL: Pearls can be formed inside clams, mussels, or oysters.

POTATO FISH: The potato grouper is also called a potato bass. Its outside looks rather like a baked potato.

PUFFERFISH: There are more than one hundred and twenty different kinds of pufferfish. They puff up their bodies when an enemy scares them.

SEA HORSE: There are twenty-five kinds of sea horses. These tiny fish have horse-shaped heads.

TIGER SHARK: Young tiger sharks have dark stripes. The stripes fade away as they grow older and larger.

Debbie Dadey

is an award-winning children's book author who has written more than 175 traditionally published books. She is best known for her series The Adventures of the Bailey School Kids, written with Marcia Thornton Jones. Debbie lives with her husband and two dogs in Sevierville, Tennessee. She is not a mermaid . . . yet.